The Power of Love

By

D.D. Bennett
(also known as Debra D. Bennett)

Chapter 1

"Good Morning" Darya sang as she stood at the bottom of the staircase clothed in her red, mini silk robe. Her hair was pulled back in a ponytail, and it bounced as her head gently, vibrated from the excitement that was bubbling in the pit of her stomach. She was wearing the diamond studs Jeffery gave her on their first wedding anniversary. They were young, in love and ready to conquer the world. Nothing could stop them. Well, that was until life sunk her teeth into them. It was as if she latched on to the very fiber of their beings, ripping into their minds, bodies, souls and spirits. She wore them down and stripped them bare, until there was very little left. Darya tugged at the tiny stone pinned to her soft, brown lobe. Yes, they were small; the earrings were merely fragments of a carat. But Darya didn't care about the size or monetary value. No, she absolutely adored them. For her, these tiny specks represented a happier, much simpler time that was filled with love and passion. Even though, since that day Jeffery has showered her with glitzy jewelry and designer handbags; Darya's favorite gift, the thing that caused her eyes to glisten, were the tiny ¼ carat earrings that she wore with pride.

Darya glided over to the middle of the kitchen towards the island. She hummed a little tune as she grabbed the glass vase from under the sink. She placed one-half dozen fresh, yellow tulips in the tall, cylinder shaped container and placed the opening under the running facet. Darya loved fresh flowers, especially tulips. She considered them to be such elegant flowers. The long sleek stem. The wide, tender pedals. There was no prettier flower in the world, at least in her mind. She smiled as she gently placed the arrangement in the center of the counter. Darya felt that the yellow complimented the white, quartz counter top nicely. "Dah, da-da dah" she sang as she placed the pan-seared toast on a plate next to some fresh, colorful berries. She unfolded the wooden tray base that was in the pantry and grabbed the cream colored, woven basket from the top shelf. Darya smiled as she placed the delicious vittles inside the rectangular shaped box. She was so engrossed in thought that she didn't hear Jeffrey until he made his final descent down the stairs, landing firmly on the hard, ceramic tile that covered the kitchen floor. Darya spun around in excitement, with tray in hand. But her bright, beautiful smile slowly faded away as she stared at her husband in bewilderment. "Wh- where are you going?"

"Oh didn't I tell you? I have a meeting with Elder Michaels this morning".

"Great." Darya mumbled under her breath. She threw the breakfast tray onto the island. She was furious. *How could he be so inconsiderate?* She thought to herself. Darya, who absolutely treasured sleep, got up early to make Jeffery his favorite breakfast. They both had been crazy busy with work and church that they hardly saw each other. Breakfast was coffee on the go. Lunch occurred at the desk. And dinner? Well, that was mostly takeout. Darya thought today, of all days, she would cook. She would give Jeffery all the things she had deprived him of over the past twelve months.

"Oh babe, I'm sorry. I thought I told you." Disappointment covered Darya's face. Jeffery felt a sting in his chest. He looked down at the plate of food in front of him, "But you know I can't leave without this?" He grabbed a slice of French toast from the plate and stuffed it into his mouth. He quickly grabbed the glass of cool, smooth liquid to wash down the lump of bread in his throat. He smacked his thick, luscious lips as he rubbed his tummy. "Thanks Babe, that was delicious" he said with a boyish grin across his face. "You're the greatest."

"But-" Jeffery leaned over and kissed his wife gently on her soft, full lips.

He looked at his watch. "Sorry, no time to talk. I'm running late. I promise I'll make it up to you. Love you." Jeffery reached over, grabbed his keys from the counter and bolted out of the door. Darya reached her hand into her pocket and pulled out a small wrapped gift box. Her finger traced the pearl white ribbon that outlined the package. Tears began to fall slowly from her almond shaped brown eyes.

"Happy anniversary" she whispered. Darya threw the box on the table and started to walk up the stairs when the phone rang. "Hello?" she whispered in a faint voice as she fought back the tears that stung the back of her eyes.

"Hi Darya, I hate to disturb you on your day off" A smile covered Darya's face at the sound of the familiar deep voice on the other end.

"Hi Fred" Darya looked around the huge empty kitchen. She was so disheartened by the site. Never had she imagined she would be home, alone on one of the supposedly happiest days of her life. Darya frowned at the thought. "Don't worry about it. I wasn't doing anything anyway. What's up?" Fred informed Darya that a new consultant was starting and that he wanted her to work with him on a new, high profile project. He told her that it was imperative that they begin working on the project immediately, so she would need to come back early from her vacation. Darya was taking time off so that she and Jeffery could spend some time together. And since it was their eighth anniversary, she figured this would be the perfect time. But obviously Jeffery was too busy to spend time with her, and she would rather be working than sitting home alone. So she agreed to come in and committed to be there within the hour.

Chapter 2

As Jeffery approached the stoplight, he realized he forgot his portfolio. Irritated by his unreliable memory, he looped around the block in order to go back to the house. He had been so busy lately with the church that he would forget his head if it wasn't attached.

Jeffery had been pastoring for five years now and, to his dismay, it wasn't getting any easier. Sure, he knew ministry was not easy. He was a pastor's kid. And he witnessed first hand the toil ministry could take on a person. His dad pastored the same church for 40 years, and his life was the church. If he wasn't in a revival meeting, he was in a church meeting or on some consultative call. It was like he worked 24-hours a day, 7-days a week. But despite the long days and late nights, his dad loved being a pastor. His face lit up every time he talked about the goodness of God, and His undying love for His people. Jeffery knew his dad was called to pastor, and since he was a young boy, he felt the same burning desire. Unfortunately, everyone couldn't understand it, not even in his family. He chuckled to himself as he reflected on his grandmother's response to his declaration about pastoring. "Jeffery, boy hush dat foolishness. Shucks, I'm sho dat deh is some stuff yo deddy put in yo head." She chided. Big Mamma Pearline was an acquired taste. She thought she was an authority on everything and made it a point to let everyone know it. "Theh is mo'ta life den go'n to chuch. Ya still yun. Go out. Have fun. Enjoy life. Ya got time for all that preach'n bidness when ya olda." Her words cut him like a knife. After that, he doubted his calling. Maybe he was being silly. What sane person wants to be preacher anyway? Jeffery wrestled with the idea of pastoring up until is senior year of high school. He thought back to the day God gave him freedom. He was about 17 years old and in mental anguish about his future. Jeffery only wanted to fulfill his destiny, but what was that? Normal boys his age were focused on college, parties and girls, but not him. He found all of that to be trivial; he wanted something more meaningful. Jeffery sat slumped over the kitchen table, his face resting gently in his hands. His dad, Jeffery Senior, came inside the house after spending most of the day outside, tinkering with his old, pick-up truck. The heavy screen door made a loud smacking sound as it fell hard against the wooden doorframe.

"What's the matter Jeff?" His dad threw his dirty, sweaty cap on the table as he walked over to the fridge. He grabbed the pitcher of ice tea and poured the smooth, crisp liquid into a huge cup. The cubes popped as if they were being shocked by electricity. Jeffery Senior plopped into the chair next to him. Sweat dripping from his large, round face. Jeffery peered between his long, slender fingers. His dad could see that he was in despair, but he had no idea as to why. Jeffery sat quietly. He wouldn't even lift up his head. "Well, you gonna answer me boy?" He dad's voice darkened. Jeffrey sat up in the chair.

"No-nothing."

"Don't lie to me son. Something's wrong, so let's hear it."

Jeffrey took a deep breath. He was nervous. His grandmother already told him he was crazy. What if his dad said the same thing? He would be devastated.

"Well, I'm- I'm trying to figure out what I want to do." Feeling defeated, Jeffery lowered himself in the chair.

"Do about what?"

"About life. I'm trying to decide what I want to do with it." His dad nodded his head as he listened. "And, well . . . I don't know. I can't figure out what I'm meant to do."

His dad took a long, deep breath. "Well son, what do you like doing?" Jeffrey looked down at the dark, brown cherry wood table. He shrugged his shoulders.

"I don't' know."

"Well, sure you do. What can't you wait to do when the sun comes up? What is that one thing you'd rather do than eat and sleep, cuz we both know how much you love to do that." Jeffery chuckled.

"Yeah, I do love to eat . . .and sleep." He paused and looked at his dad, seriousness in his eyes. "Pop, I want to do what you do." His dad sat up in his chair.

"What do you mean?"

"Well, I want to be a pastor." His dad started to nod his head again.

"Why?" Jeffery had a blank look on his face. Sensing his bewilderment, his dad continued. "Son, pastoring is a serious job, not something to be taken lightly and definitely not something that is for the faint in heart. If you want to pastor, that's great. But you can't do it because I do it. That's not enough. So I'm going to ask you again. Why?" Jeffery sat there for a moment. Trying to find the words to say.

"Well pop, I feel like that is what I was born to do." His dad smiled and started to nod his head again. "I look forward to going to church. Reading the Word. Hearing from God. I love telling other people about His goodness." He stopped. "Pop, does that make me weird?"

"Weird?"

"Yeah, grandma said that wasn't normal." Jeffery's dad took another deep breath and rolled his eyes.

"Lord that woman." He said annoyingly. "Boy, in life people won't always agree with things you say or do. And that's okay, as long as God is alright with your decisions. But you're gonna have to be comfortable with that. If not, you'll never be all that God wants you to be." His dad leaned over towards him. Small beads of sweat started to fall from his dark, sunburned brow. He reached over and placed his large, calloused hands on the back of Jeffery's neck. "Junior, I believe that God has a call on your life. Since you were a small child, I could see the glory of God all over you. You are going to do great things for Him, if you let Him have full control. Don't let anyone stop you from walking in your destiny son." Tears began to fall from Jeffery's eyes. "Let's pray for your future." Jeffery stretched out his hand and placed it on his father's arm. As his dad prayed, Jeffery felt such peace, it was like something he'd never experienced before. From that day forward, Jeffery stood on his conviction to pastor. A smile curled his lips as he reflected on that life-changing experience he shared with his dad around the kitchen table that Saturday morning.

As Jeffery pulled into the driveway, a rush of joy filled his heart.

"This is what I was called to do," he muttered to himself. After putting the car in park, he opened the door, sprinted out of the seat and up the steps. Once inside, he spotted his bag in the chair by the kitchen table. As he walked over to pick it up, his eye caught a glimpse of something. Jeffery picked up the small, neatly wrapped package from the table. As he rotated the tiny box in his hand, he marveled at how smooth the paper was. It was like touching satin.

The sound of clacking heels broke his concentration. "Babe what's this?" Darya was dressed in a black tee length fitted skirt and a pinstriped shirt with white cuffs. She was putting in her white, pearl earrings to match the string of pearls that hung gently around her neck. Her hair was pulled back in a bun, which gave her a very professional, yet sophisticated look.

"Nothing of importance" she stated coolly during her final descent into the kitchen. Jeffery looked at her attire and gave her a puzzled look.

"I thought you were taking some time off?"

"For what?" Her words were as cold as the ice that ran through her veins.

"What's wrong with you?" He snapped.

 "Nothing" she snarled as she rolled her eyes. Darya reached passed him and grabbed her keys from the table. "Fred called. I have to go in. I don't know what time I'll be back, so don't wait on me for dinner." And just like that Darya was out the door.

"Uhhh, what just happened?" he muttered to himself as the door slammed shut behind her. Surrounded by silence, Jeffery stood in the kitchen with a dazed look on his face. He was thoroughly confused. She was in such a delightful mood earlier. What could have caused her mood to change so abruptly? As he pondered the morning's events, he glanced at the clock. "Shoot. I'm gonna be late." Jeffery rolled his eyes in frustration. Oh how he hated being late. He quickly grabbed his briefcase from the chair and darted out the door.

Jeffery couldn't understand what was wrong with Darya. She seemed so disgruntled. He admitted that things had been difficult between them the past few years, but nothing warranted this sort of behavior. As he drove down the busy street he tried to figure out where it all went wrong. Yes he had been distracted with the church, but he was fulfilling his divine call. God called him to be a pastor, and for that reason he had to give one hundred percent. He drove into the church parking lot and turned off the engine. "This is just a distraction," he muttered to himself. "And distraction only leads to defeat."

Jeffery got of out the car and walked up the steps of the brown, brick building. He was the first Black Pastor this church had in its fifty years of existence. It was groundbreaking . . . revolutionary.   The people needed to see that he was seriously dedicated to building this ministry.

As he walked into the administrative offices, a huge smile covered his face at the distinct shrill of his administrative assistant's voice.

"Good Morning Pastor"

"Good Morning Rose" Jeffery chortled as he passed her desk.

"Your first appointment is here," she said as she nodded her head in the direction of his office. Rose handed him a stack of letters and phone messages, which Jeffery accepted graciously.

"Thank you," Jeffery walked into his office. Elder Michaels was seated casually in one of the wingback leather chairs. He had on a cream colored linen suit, and freshly shined tan leather shoes. His salt and pepper hair was neatly cut, and his greenish colored eyes lit up when he saw Jeffery. "Good Morning Elder" Jeffery said with a huge boyish grin on his face.

"Good Morning Pastor" the two men shook hands as they continued to exchange pleasantries.

"Alright let's get down to business shall we?" Jeffery closed the door softly behind him so that he and Elder Michaels could discuss business privately.

Chapter 3

"Good Morning Darya."

"Good Morning Mary." Mary had been Darya's assistant for two years, and was very proud of that fact that she knew everything there was to know about her boss. She was always two steps ahead of Darya and never failed to have everything ready for her exactly when she needed it.

"Mr. Cummings would like to see you immediately and all of your messages are on your desk waiting for you."

Darya gave Mary a huge grin. Mary thought it was because of Darya's warm spirit. But Darya's smile was more of a relief than mere appreciation for a job well done. "Thanks dear."

"Um, quick question for you." Darya's head popped up as she placed her purse on the desk.

"Ok, shoot."

"What are you doing here? Isn't it your anniversary?" Without thought, Darya fell backwards, landing comfortably in the chair. For the first time, Mary could not read her boss' expression. Darya was tired. That she could decipher. But there was something else. Something more. She just couldn't put her finger on it.

"Hmph, it's no fun celebrating by yourself."

"What happened?"

Darya rolled her eyes, "No dear you're not asking the right question. It's not what happened, it's what didn't happen." As Darya recounted the morning's events Mary stood in the doorway with her mouth opened in a state of shock. She had met Jeffery a few times at company functions, and he came by the office a couple of times to see Darya. She thought they made such a handsome couple. It hurt her heart to see them in this type of predicament. Mary could see the pain in Darya's face. She quickly grabbed the box of tissue that was on the shelf and handed them to Darya. Mary enjoyed having a boss who was a Christian. She didn't have to endure crude language or ungodly conversations. Darya was a true Believer, and she admired that about her.

"Darya, you have to pull yourself together. Every marriage goes through this type of....funk, if you will. It doesn't mean your marriage is over, and what man doesn't forget an anniversary? God will work it out, you'll see."

"Yeah, that's what *they* say." Darya grabbed the file from her desk and headed down to Fred's office. The hallway was neatly decorated with beautiful abstract paintings. The colors elicited feelings of warmth and serenity. Darya desperately needed to feel this. Her heart was broken, and despite Mary's encouragement, she couldn't help but feel empty, alone and betrayed.

"Hi Fred, Mary said that you wanted to see me." Fred stood to his feet as Darya entered the room. His grey pants were baggy, and rested below his protruding belly. Fred had a warm, pleasant face, one that made a person feel relaxed and at ease, almost instantly. This is probably why he was always selected to play Santa Claus at the company's holiday party. Fred had on a white crisp oxford shirt with the initials FJC embroidered on the sleeves. A red tie with specks of blue, yellow and black hung tightly around his neck, and Darya couldn't help but wonder about his color selection.

"Yes, Darya, I would like you to meet the newest addition to our team, Chase Alexander Peyton III." As Fred motioned his hand, a young man slowly rose to his feet, revealing his height and breadth. His hazel eyes sparkled as he reached out to shake Darya's hand.

"Hi Chase, it's very nice to meet you."

"Chase this is Darya Elaine Drukker. Darya here is our top consultants in the firm. And don't let that cool demeanor fool you, this lady is a real tiger." Although Darya was disturbed by the title, she smiled graciously. In her heart she was sure Fred was trying to pay her a compliment, but it didn't feel that way. Tigers were vicious animals, and she was anything but vicious. Was she passionate? Yes. Slightly intense? . . . at times . . . okay, most times. But ferocious? No . . . not really. Okay, maybe sometimes, but definitely not all the time.

"Hi Darya, nice to meet you as well." The warm, dark timber of Chase's voice cut through her thoughts like a knife. She immediately felt chills trickle down her spine like beads of cool water. Fred motioned Darya to take the vacant seat next to Chase. Butterflies filled her stomach as the scent of his cologne filled her nostrils. His dark features accented his caramel colored complexion. He wore a black, tailored suit with a light green shirt and a black and green tie. The attire . . . the color choice . . . it was definitely on point and very appealing. And very unnerving for Darya. Sitting beside him, she grew tense and felt ill at ease. She twisted in her seat, trying to make herself comfortable. But it didn't work. She couldn't relax. Well, that was until her eyes beheld the glittering band of gold that donned his large ring finger. Darya blew a huge sigh of relief and slouched back slightly in her seat. She grimaced at her reaction. *What was that all about?* She thought to herself. Never had a man had such an effect on her . . . not even Jeffery.

Chapter 4

It was getting late and Jeffery's last appointment was gone. As he sat at his desk, his mind went back to the early morning fiasco with Darya. "God please give me a clue as to what's going on." At that moment Rose came into the office.

"Ok Pastor, I'm about to leave for the day." Jeffery's train of thought was broken by Rose's intrusion. He looked at her and gave her a faint smile.

"Thank you for your hard work Rose" Rose smiled at the compliment, but then a look of concern swept over her face as she studied the countenance of her disheveled pastor.

"Is everything okay Pastor Drukker?" He nodded his head gently.

"Yeah, just tired that's all." She smiled at him and said,

"Well you can get plenty rest, AFTER you take the misses out for your anniversary" Jeffery's head snapped up.

"Anniversary!!! That's why she was so irritated with me. How could I be such an idiot?" Rose's eyes widened,

"Please don't tell me you forgot your OWN anniversary?" Jeffery squinched his face and said in a deep voice,

"Ok then, I won't tell you."

Rose shook her head. "Pastor, how could you?"

Jeffery jumped up from his desk and started packing his things together. "I didn't do it on purpose. I've just been so busy...it slipped my mind"

"Well you better get going. The mall is closing shortly and you will need something pretty and expensive to keep you out of the dog house tonight"

How could I be so stupid? Jeffery thought to himself. *Darya was upset because I forgot about our anniversary*. He had been so preoccupied that the date slipped his mind. In his defense, it was marked on the calendar so technically he didn't forget . . . well, not really. He just got sidetracked. As he perused the aisle of the department store, he thought about Darya. He loved her, with all of his heart. He simply needed a way to convey it.

Jeffery approached the jewelry section. *All women love jewelry.* He thought to himself. As he stood in front of the glass display case, his eye caught a glimpse of a beautiful, vintage diamond pendant. It was cushion shaped and encased in white gold and yellow diamonds. The luminescent gems sparkled in the florescent lighting, giving it a regal appearance. It was fit for royalty and perfect for his queen. Convinced this would be the perfect expression of his love, he immediately signaled the associate to make the purchase.

On his way to the house, Jeffery picked up a dozen, long stemmed red roses and dinner from Darya's favorite Italian restaurant. He set the table for two and lit scented candles throughout the house. If she wanted romance, he was determined to give it to her. Tonight, he would show Darya how much she meant to him and give her the night of her life.

Chapter 5

Chase pulled his sleek, black luxury sedan into the driveway. As he pressed the button on the garage remote, he let out a deep sigh. The day had been very strenuous, and the only thing he had strength to do right now was thank God it was over. As he slowly made his way into the garage his mind replayed the day's events. The pressure of starting a new job, the nervousness that gripped him in the pit of his stomach with each encounter. Chase turned off the engine and slid out of the car. Before closing the door he reached over to the passenger side and grabbed his brown, leather briefcase. He made his way up the gray cement steps, and slowly turned the gold doorknob. He stepped over the threshold and gently closed the door behind him.

"Hey hon I'm home" he sang as he walked into the living room, dropping his briefcase in the corner. His wife was curled up on the couch reading a book. Chase didn't know what she was reading, but by the looks of it, she was pretty enthralled. Stephanie gave a slight wave in acknowledgement, but her eyes didn't part from the pages that rested on her fingertips. Chase began untying his tie as he dragged his tired body up the stairs. He was so exhausted. All he wanted was a hot shower and a bed.

Stephanie was pulling back the covers when Chase came out of the bathroom.

"So, how was your first day?"

"It was good. Tiring, but good" he beamed. "My boss, Fred, seems to be really cool...I think I'm really going to like there."

"Well that's good. I'm happy for you." After they both were in the bed, Stephanie reached over to turn off her lamp. Chase laid still for a moment. As she moved her body, he could feel the cool satin material from her gown against his warm skin. The sound of her breathing, and her sweet perfumed scent that filled his nostrils made him want her. He gently rolled his large frame towards her, extending his strong arms to caress her body.
"Steph" he said in a deep, husky voice. As he softly kissed her face and neck, his hand slowly slid down her gown and made its way up her leg.

"Chase, not tonight" She muttered in an irritated tone. But Chase was consumed with passion. He wanted Stephanie, needed her. It had been months since they had been intimate and he longed for the touch of his wife. As he continued to caress her body and kiss her neck, she jumped up. "Good Lord, not tonight" she growled "Or don't you understand English anymore?" Hurt by her reaction, Chase pulled away from her. He quietly rolled over, turned off his lamp and went to sleep.

Stephanie woke up to the sound of birds chirping. The sun was bright and she wished to herself that she had purchased the blackout curtains Chase wanted a while back. She was a morning person, but lately she had felt drained, borderline lethargic. As Stephanie rolled out of the bed, she noticed that Chase was gone. She grabbed her robe from the chaise and slowly walked down the stairs. The plush carpet was soft beneath her feet. The pleasant aroma of freshly brewed coffee filled the air. Chase was sitting at the kitchen table drinking a cup of coffee as he flipped through the pages of the local newspaper. His white dressed shirt hugged the curves of his muscular arms, and the silver chromed watch that clung loosely to his thick wrist complemented his bronzed skin. He peeped over the paper as Stephanie glided into the kitchen.

Chase had been up since five o'clock that morning. He was so frustrated by Stephanie's rejection that he could hardly sleep. He couldn't figure out why she disliked him so. What did he do to her? Why was she rejecting him? When he got up out of the bed, Stephanie was sound asleep. He looked at her lying there, so peacefully as if everything was okay. But nothing had been fine between them for a long time. He was just going through the motions. He wasn't even sure if he still loved her. He pulled on his sweats, grabbed his sneakers and gently closed the door behind him. Chase grabbed his jacket and phone on the way out the door. The cool air whipped across his face as he jogged down the well lit sidewalk. He loved to run. It was his method for clearing his head, and boy did he have a lot he needed to think through.

When he came into the house, it was still dark. He threw the keys onto the table and showered in the hall bathroom so that he wouldn't disturb Stephanie. He kept replaying the previous night's events over and over in his mind. Some how he had to find a way to make his marriage work. The only question was how.

"Babe?"

"Yeah?" Stephanie muttered as she poured herself a hot cup of java.

"Let's go away." Stephanie crinkled up her nose. Chase could tell by her expression that she was not very impressed with the idea. He walked over to her, and placed his arms around her waist. "I know how much you like the beach. We can get an oceanfront hotel room and just hang out, me and you with no distractions." His breath was warm against her ear, as his lips brushed the nape of her neck.

"But you hate the beach" she chuckled.

"But for you, I'm willing to go. Would that make you happy?" Stephanie stepped forward and turned around to face him.

"Work is busy right now, and not to mention, you just started a new job. I don't think going away would be a good idea right now." Stephanie kissed him softly on the cheek. "I have to get ready for work." She said as she stepped around him to leave the kitchen. Disappointedly Chase put on his sport coat, grabbed his keys and headed out the door.

Chapter 6

The screeching alarm caused Darya to jump up. "Oh my Lord what time is it?" Groggy, Jeffery leaned over to turn off the alarm.

"It's six thirty." Darya climbed out of the bed frantically.

"I have an eight o'clock meeting this morning!" Jeffery placed his feet on the warm plush carpet. He ran his hands over his face and looked around the room as if disoriented. He grabbed his pajama pants from the floor and poked his head inside of the bathroom. The entire room was filled with steam from the shower.

"Do you want me to fix you something for breakfast?"

"Um, a bagel and some cappuccino" Darya shouted back over the roaring stream of water.   After she turned off the faucet, she stepped onto the burgundy mat. She wrapped a towel around her small frame and strolled out of the bathroom. *Hhhmmm. What to wear? What to wear?* Darya walked over to her closet and began to scan her clothes. She had a very important business meeting with the Vice President of a large banking corporation. Today was the day she had to bring it. She chose a royal blue suit and a cream camisole. Her hair was pinned back in a twist and the thin, gold chain that hung from her neck complemented her color choice. The delicious aroma of vanilla roasted coffee beans was so thick it could be tasted. As she floated down the stairs, she felt like a cartoon character who was being carried away by a delightful fragrance. Once in the kitchen, Darya grabbed the hot bagel slices from the toaster and covered it with strawberry cream cheese. As she poured the cappuccino in her travel mug, she thought about how in love she and Jeffery used to be. How she loved being around him and how good he always made her feel. They did everything together, and at the end of the day they would always spend time talking about their day. He always made her feel as if she was the only person in the world who mattered.

Jeffery glanced at her, and as if he was reading her mind he said,

"You know, things have been really hectic lately, and we haven't spent any time together in a really long time." Darya was frozen. She couldn't move. Couldn't meet his eyes. He had no idea how powerful those simple words were. The truthfulness of his statement struck a chord in her heart. She fought to keep back the tears that stung her big brown eyes. Jeffery turned to face his beautiful, young wife. He walked over to her slowly, and put his arms around her slender waist. "What do you say about us taking off . . . no work, no church, just you and me?" Darya couldn't believe her ears. Spend time together, her and Jeffery? She marveled at the idea, but would it actually come to pass? Oh how she wanted to spend time with her husband, to be lost in his love and engulfed in his passion. Darya looked at him, her eyes gleaming, full of hope and love.

"I- I would like that" she stammered. "I would like that very much."

Darya was above the clouds. She and Jeffery had decided they would leave that afternoon for an extended weekend.

After her meeting, she hurried to her office to drop-off some files and rearrange some appointments. Darya was a shrewd businesswoman, but Jeffery's news that morning put her somewhat off kilter. She tried with all her might to focus on the conversation with the VP, but all she could see and hear was Jeffery. Yes, God had finally answered her prayers, and she was getting her husband back. Oh how her heart sang at the thought.

"Well, it looks like someone had a good anniversary after all." Mary was all smiles. She was a hopeless romantic so she was more than ready to hear the juicy details of their romantic evening.

"Oh my! I am so excited. Guess where Jeffery's taking me?"

"Where?" She giggled with excitement.

"Uhhmmm, my husband, yes the wonderful man that I married, is taking me to the resort this weekend." All smiles. Bubbling over with excitement.

 "Wwwooowww"

"Yes, a-" Darya was interrupted by the chirping of her office phone. "Hold that thought." She grabbed the receiver, clearing her throat before introducing herself to the caller. Mary leaned over Darya's desk like a wide-eyed schoolgirl. She couldn't help but be sucked in by Darya's excitement. It was magnetic.

As Darya spun around in her chair to converse with the person on the other end, Mary checked her hair and make-up in the mirror that hung on the wall across the room. Mary was one who always cared about her looks. Nails always freshly manicured, and trendy outfits that hugged her curves just right. She patted the sides of her hair and smiled at herself in appreciation. When she heard the click of the receiver, she spun around in anticipation only to find water filled eyes staring helplessly up at her.
Mary caught her breath. "What-"

Darya put her hand up in protest. "I don't want to talk about it." She grabbed a couple sheets of tissue from the box on her desk. "Can you just give me a moment? And hold all calls for now."

Mary nodded her head and walked out of Darya's office, closing the door gently behind her. Darya put her head on the desk as she sobbed quietly, recounting her conversation with Jeffery.

"Hey Babe, I hate to do this, but something's come up and I need to cancel our trip."

"What?! Why?! You promised!"

"I know, but there's a leak in the pipes at the church and now the basement is flooded."

"Okay, but last I checked, you weren't a plumber, so what does that have to do with you?"

"No, I'm not the plumber. But I am the Pastor, and I need to fix it."

"But can't it wait? Or better yet, can't one of the Elders handle it . . . that's what they are there for, right?"

"Honey, it just doesn't look right for me to leave right now. Besides I have an obligation to the church. This has to take precedence."

"Yeah, but what about your obligation to me?" Darya whispered as she hung up the phone. She tried. She was trying. But why was this so hard? She always did the right thing. Her entire life she always did what was expected of her. So why was this happening to her? Why was she being punished?

"Darya?" Darya's head shot up at the sound of her name. She told Mary she didn't want to talk to anyone. No one really did mean no one.
"I'm sorry, I didn't mean to barge in, but your assistant wasn't at her desk. Is everything okay?"

Darya quickly wiped the tears from her eyes. She did not like for people to see her in such a vulnerable state. Crying? Never, especially not in front of a stranger. "I'm fine. What can I help you with?"

Chase sat in the chair across from Darya. He recognized pain and rejection when he saw it.

"I know you don't know me that well." He paused, unsure of what to say, or more specifically, how to say it. "But I want you to know that I'm here for you, if you need me to be."

So warm and so sincere, how could she be mean? But no matter how much she wanted to let him in, she couldn't find the words to speak. Opening up was never her strong suit. "Thanks, but I'm fine." She stammered.

Chase knew she was lying, but he did not want to pressure her into doing anything she did not want to do. He gave her a faint smile and nodded before getting up and walking out of the office.

Chapter 7

Work had been crazy. Deadlines. Endless meetings. Darya had been so consumed with projects, that she had little time to focus on her problems with Jeffery. Jeffery. Both of them had been so busy lately that they saw very little of each other. Part of that, of course, was intentional. Communication wasn't the greatest between them. And lately they seemed to talk at each other verses talking to each other. The thought of it all hurt Darya to her heart. She loved Jeffery, but she needed more than he was giving her. Sure she tried telling him on more than one occasion, but he didn't seem to understand. Somehow he would always interpret her pleas for time and attention as her wanting more sexual intimacy.

Darya sat at her computer, gazing at the screen. It was late and words were starting to run together. She couldn't think any more. She didn't want to think anymore. *Ugh, forget it. I'm done. Completely zapped.* She had worked late all week. She decided that she would sleep in tomorrow. She sent a couple of documents to the printer and shutdown her computer. As she drifted down the hall, she heard a deep, muffled voice in the distance. Darya tried not to listen to the conversation that was taking place, but she couldn't help it.

"I was hoping we could spend some time together tonight. Just you and me. I know th-" Although Darya couldn't hear the person on the other end, she sensed that this person was not too impressed. "Uh huh . . . . yes, I understand. That's fine. See you then." As Chase hung up the phone, he swore under his breath. Guilt had immediately set in. He tried never to curse. But lately, he was so frustrated that it seemed to spill out before he could even stop it.

"It's none of your business Darya. Keep walking." She muttered to herself. But Chase was her friend, and he was upset. How could she not at least check to make sure everything was okay? Reluctantly, Darya detoured from the printer and knocked gently on Chase's door, which was half opened. She peeked her head inside, and saw Chase sitting at his desk with his hands covering his face. He looked tired. Emotionally drained.

"Hey, is everything okay?" She stammered. As his gaze lifted, she slowly walked into his office. "I was on my way to the printer and noticed your light was on." She felt dishonest because she actually heard him on the phone first. Because of that, she couldn't look him directly in the eyes. So she glanced around the office instead. "It's really late . . . I thought I was the only one insane enough to be here at this hour." She smiled, trying to lighten the mood and fade away the bitterness and frustration in the air.

"Yeah, I'm good." He leaned back in his chair as he fumbled around with a gold ink pen on his desk. "I was just trying to wrap things up. My plan is to take some time off so I can concentrate on the Misses." Darya winced from the sting of jealousy that hit her.

"Wow, must be nice." Darya's face went pale.

"What? What is it?" Chase's eyes rested on Darya's face. He was actually afraid to look away. Even though he had no idea as to why.

At that point, Darya couldn't do it any longer. She was naturally a strong woman. She relied on no one. She could hold her own. But she was so tired. Between work and arguments with Jeffery, she honestly couldn't control her demeanor any longer. Her brown eyes glistened as they filled with water, and although she tried to fight back the tears, they streamed down her face.

Chase got-up and walked over to the empty chair across from her. "Darya, what is it? Did I say something to upset you?"

Darya stared helplessly at the floor. "Yes . . . I mean no" shaking her head from side-to-side. "I'm sorry, it's not you . . . it's me. I'm sorry, I better go." She tried to stand, but Chase's hand was on her shoulder.

"Darya, I'm your friend. What's wrong?" In that moment, Darya felt closer to Chase than to any other person in the world. That would include her husband. Darya and Chase had spent a lot of time together at work, and she enjoyed every minute of it. He always listened intently to every story she told, and he even laughed at her corny jokes. They talked about everything. Well, almost everything. Although they shared stories about their personal lives, they never talked about their marriages. Sure, he knew Jeffery existed, and she new Stephanie was there, but they never discussed them. In that moment Darya wondered why.

"Nothing, it's hormones." Darya chuckled lightly. Chase felt as if someone just punched him in the gut.

"Oh, I'm-I guess congratulations are in order." Darya crinkled her nose as her eyebrows drew in closer. Chase stood. Fidgeting. Why was he bothered by the news? Surely this is the natural progression of things.

"Oh . . . oh . . . no, no" she shook her head incessantly. "Do you think? I'm not . . . do I look pregnant to you?" Her eyes wide with shock and horror as she placed her hand over her lower abdomen.

"No, no you don't. You said hormones, so-"

"So, you immediately jumped to me being pregnant? Geez, I mean most people would think I was referring to it being that time of the month or something. Who automatically thinks pregnancy?!" Chase had no idea his comment would spark such a reaction.

"Doesn't every married woman want a baby?"

"Doesn't every married woman want a baby?" She mocked in a deep, clunky voice. "Um, in case you haven't notice, I'm not *every* married woman and NO I do NOT want a baby."

Darya stormed out of his office. Chase stood by the desk wondering what in the world just happened. *Hmph, well at least she stopped crying*. He chuckled at his thought. Chase turned off his computer, packed his belongings and headed out of the office. As he walked down the hall, his phone rang.

"Hey Babe!"

"Hey, listen, change of plans. Prep for this case is taking longer than I anticipated, and it's going to be late by the time I am close to being finished." There was a pause. Chase didn't know if he should say something or if Stephanie was planning to continue with her story. "I'm going to get a room at a nearby hotel for the night. I am really tired and don't feel like driving."

Chase stopped dead in his tracks. Every time they make plans, something mysteriously comes up. "Sure, I understand. We can do something another night.

"Thanks for understanding. See you tomorrow."

"See you tomorrow."

Chase ended the call and leaned back on the wall. Discouragement gripped his heart. *I don't think I can take much more of this.* As he stood there contemplating his situation with Stephanie, Darya walked out of her office. She looked at him, leaning there with that frustrated and overwhelmed look on his face again. She wondered if her outburst had anything to do with his expression.

Darya walked slowly toward him. "Hey, you" jabbing him in the shoulder. "I'm sorry about my female breakdown a while ago." Chase turned to look at her, pain in his eyes. Darya stopped. It was enough to make her heart break into a thousand pieces.

"Chase?"

"I'm tired."

Darya searched his face for answers. *Was it me?* She thought to herself. "What's wrong?"

"Have you ever loved someone . . . and every attempt to connect with them gets shot down? Do you know what it's like when the person you love constantly rejects your love?" Darya knew that feeling all too well. All she could do was shake her head in agreement. "I've tried. I'm trying. But I can't keep torturing myself." Chase looked down at Darya. Her eyes so warm and tender. "You would never do that would you? You would appreciate your man." Chase traced the side of Darya's cheek with his fingertip. His hand so warm and soft. It sent chills down Darya's spine. "Hhmmm, Jeffery doesn't know how lucky he is."

"Do you want to talk about it?" Darya whispered. But before Chase could respond, her phone rang. It was Jeffery. "Um, sorry. Excuse me." Darya felt nervous, but she couldn't figure out why. She was doing nothing wrong. "Hello?"

"Hey, where are you? It's late." Darya looked up at Chase. Should she explain that she was consoling her friend who was heartbroken about his hard-hearted wife? Would he understand? Would he even care? Part of her wanted to tell him, just to see if it would elicit some sort of emotion. But she put the idea out of her mind since things had been pretty strained between them lately.

"I'm sorry, I had to work late. I'm actually wrapping things up now and about to head out. I will give you a call when I'm in the car and on my way. Bye."

Darya looked at Chase, "I'm sorry, I-"

He raised his hand in protest to her explanation. "No need to explain. I understand. You better get home."

As they walk towards the elevator, everything got quiet. It was as if they were afraid to speak. They rode the elevator to the parking garage. It was completely empty. Not a vehicle in sight. Normally Darya would be a little uneasy, but tonight she felt safe. Chase walked Darya to her car. Darya fought against the schoolgirl giddiness that tried to creep up inside her. *This is not a date, and he is not a crush. He is my co-worker and there is nothing going on here.* Darya thought to herself. She threw her things in the backseat. Without thinking, she reached out to grab the door handle, not realizing that Chase was about to open the door for her. In that moment their hands touched, sending electricity throughout her body.

"Oh sorry, I didn't realize-" she stammered nervously, wondering if he felt it too.

"Hey, I'm a gentleman, this is what I do." His smile wide and bright, causing his entire face to light up.

Darya said thanks and got into the car. Chase leaned in with one hand laid casually on top of her silver sedan. For a moment he seemed to be in deep thought, as if he was trying to find the words to say. Darya waited eagerly for him to speak. But in a flash, the look was gone. He simply gave her a polite smile and closed the door. As he walked away, Darya exhaled deeply. "Be careful Darya," she whispered to herself. "You are playing with fire."

Chapter 8

"What am I doing?" *Chase* muttered to himself. "She's married. Heck, I'm married." The cool, crisp Fall breeze whipped across the damp, taunt shirt that gently hugged his muscles, sending a slight chill down his spine. Music blaring. Drums blazing. Chaotic rhythms and rhymes, all bringing solace to his cluttered mind. He loved his wife, even if he was no longer in love with her. With everything in him, he wanted to make her happy. He just didn't know how to do it. Every time he tried to get close, she pulled away. It felt so good to be around someone who didn't retreat from his touch, whose eyes lit up when he smiled. Being with her was so much easier. It wasn't hard. There was no struggle. Didn't he deserve easy? Hadn't he suffered long enough? The more he thought, the faster he ran. It was as if electricity was running through his body, fueling him. Down the street. Around the corner. He could still smell her perfume. It was sweet and tantalizing. Her skin so warm and soft, and her lips . . . Chase became so engrossed in thought that he failed to see the hole in the pavement. He stomped down with such force that his foot became wedged in-between the crack; and because his mind was so occupied, he was completely oblivious to what was about to take place. His body propelled forward and immediately jerked back, leaving him with no balance. His derrière hit the hard, rocky asphalt. The brute force caused him to scream in pain as his ankle twisted and snapped back. Chase was able to pry his foot out of the wedge. The pain was excruciating. How was he going to get home from here? A couple miles seemed like a hundred. Chase's mind was reeling. Being a former high school athlete, he recognized immediately that his joint was dislocated. He could barely focus. The pain was too intense. It was so bad that he didn't realize a car had pulled up. Nor did he see the woman running frantically towards him.

"Chase? Is that you?. . . What happened?" Darya's voice was calm, but she was trembling on the inside. The moment she saw Chase lying on the ground, it was as if her heart stopped. She didn't know why she took this route to the bakery this morning. She never came that way; it was too scenic. But when she woke up this morning, she felt . . . alive. Jeffery had an early morning meeting, so he left Darya in the bed sleeping. Normally, Darya would be irritated that Jeffery left and didn't wake her to say goodbye. But this morning was different. She woke up with a huge grin on her face and light in her eyes. She bounced around the house, dancing to her favorite song as she prepared to start the day. Darya pulled out her short-sleeved navy blue cotton-polyester blend dress that stopped right above her knees. She slid her delicate brown arms into her tan jacket and gently laid her gold chain around her neck. Since she selected the gold, dangly earrings, she decided to sweep her hair up into a ponytail. As she sat on the side of the bed to put on her shoes, she thought it would be a nice idea to bring pastries. Darya started thinking about the selection of goodies and began wondering which of the delectable items Chase would prefer. The thought of him brought a smile across her face. He was so caring, so sweet, and so . . . attentive. His warmth made her want to do nice things for him. She wanted to make him smile. With that thought in mind, she hurried out the door. Down the busy street. Through a nearby neighborhood. And now here, kneeling beside Chase.

Chase looked up. His heart melted at the sight of Darya. "Um, long story. Let's just say I thought the pavement looked lonely," he muttered with a faint laugh.

"Can you get up?"

"No, I dislocated my ankle"

"Okay. Okay. Okay." Darya's heart was racing. She was not good in crisis type situations. "I'll call 911." Darya jumped up and ran towards her car to call an ambulance. As she dialed her fingers trembled. She gave the dispatcher her location and rushed immediately to Chase's side. "Okay, the ambulance should be here shortly." Darya did her best to make Chase comfortable, but she could tell the pain was extreme and that there was very little she could do to make him feel better. "I'm sorry." Darya muttered.

"Sorry? For what?"

"Because I can't help you. I would take the pain away if I could or at least help you bear it . . . but I can't."

"Darya, you being here is enough." At that moment, their gazes locked. It was as if there was no one else in the world besides the two of them. Darya became so lost in his golden colored eyes that she didn't notice the ambulance rolling up beside them. The paramedics came and tended to Chase. Darya told Chase that she would follow them in her car and that she would call Fred to let him know what happened. As she was walking to her car, she noticed a large, black smartphone on the ground. It was near the hole and figured it belonged to Chase. She grabbed it and placed it in the passenger's seat beside her purse. *Wow! Man, it can't get much worse than this, right?* She thought to herself as she headed to the local hospital.

Chapter 9

"Here you go. Your regular . . . toast, scrambled eggs and bacon." Stephanie placed the tray of food on the nightstand beside the bed. "How is your pain?" She asked as she picked up the bottle of oxycodone the doctor prescribed. Chase pulled himself up in the bed, wincing slightly.

"The pain is tolerable . . . for now anyway." Chase looked at Stephanie. How he longed to understand her. How he desired to go back to what they used to be . . . but how? Maybe they could go back, if he could only figure out where exactly it all went wrong. He thought back to when they first met. Chase was a youth minister and Stephanie was a worship leader. Oh how he loved watching her minister through song. It was as if she glowed. And her voice, it was truly angelic. He remembered the day he mustered up the courage to ask her out. He was so nervous. In fact, he wasn't even sure she would say yes. In his mind, he was a tad bit of a cornball. Sure, he was an athlete. Played football in high school and was good enough to get a full scholarship to college. There was even talk about him being drafted into the NFL. Well, that was until he blew out his knee his junior year. But despite his talent, deep down, he felt as if he was a boring square, and definitely not her speed. In his mind he was a simple, uninteresting person whose only appealing attribute was that he was gifted with the pigskin. Whenever Chase was in the game, he dominated the field. God, how much he loved the sport. It was his future . . . his life. And when he was injured, he literally thought his world had ended. But he later came to realize that although football was his plan for his future, God had other plans for his life. One day he fully opened his heart to God and joined a local church. He then became active in campus ministry, which became his focus. To his amazement, football was not the only thing he was good at. It was evident to everyone who listened to him that God had a call on his life. A year after he asked Stephanie out, they were married. And they absolutely adored each other. He loved her, and she, he thought, loved him. But then, something went very wrong. Stephanie began drifting farther and farther away. "Steph?" He whispered gently.

"Yeah?"

"Why don't you love me anymore?" Stephanie was taken aback by his question.

"What are you talking about? What-"

"Steph, stop. Please." He whispered. "I'm- I'm tired. I can't live like this any more. I want this to work, but I can't live like this." Chase rubbed his hands across the top of his head and down his unshaven face. He looked defeated. "Things have been bad for a while now. You said it was the lack of money, so I left the ministry and got a job making more money. But, nothing has gotten better. We hardly speak and –" he stopped. The words were difficult to say. "We NEVER touch. You work all of the time, and you're always busy. But, the funny thing is, I don't feel like you're really busy. It's like you pretend to be busy so you . . . so you don't have to deal with me." His voice trailed off. He was being overtaken by his emotions.

Stephanie stood there, stunned. "Chase, . . . I – I don't know what to say."

"Then just tell me the truth. Do you still love me? Do you want this marriage to work?" At that moment the phone rang. "Don't –" but before he could finish his protest, Stephanie was out the door. After a couple of minutes Stephanie reappeared in the room.

"I – I have to go." She walked towards him slowly, refusing to give eye contact and kissed him on the forehead. "Maybe we can finish discussing tonight." As she turned to leave, Chase grabbed her hand.

"Steph, please" he pleaded. Stephanie looked at him. Tears filled her eyes. Chase pulled her down toward him. "Do you still love me?" Chase felt as if his heart was beating a million miles per minute. He feared what she might say, but he had to know.

"Chase–" Before she could complete her sentence, a melodious tune broke her train of thought. Her phone was ringing. But although she heard it, she did not see it right away. It inadvertently fell on the bed when Chase grabbed her hand. When her eyes caught a glimpse of it, she reached out to grab it. But Chase pushed it away.

"No, you're gonna talk to me"

"Chase–" The sound of his name coming from her mouth sparked a passion that he could not explain. Before he knew it, his lips were covering hers.

Stephanie woke up entangled in Chase's arms. He was a cuddler, and she was not. She maneuvered herself out of bed, managing not to wake him up. A few minutes later, Chase woke up, only to find himself in the bed alone. He fanned his hand across the sheet where she laid; it was still warm. He rolled over. Her scent covered the pillow, and he was immediately lost in it. Never had he expected this to happen. Never did he anticipate that she would concede. But she did. As he struggled to pull himself out of the bed, her phone hit the floor. When he picked it up, the screen lit up. There had to be dozens of messages from someone by the name of Tim. Chase's heart began to race. He didn't want to read them, but he couldn't help it. He couldn't keep himself from looking away. He had to know the nature of their relationship. As he read through the numerous exchanges, his heart sank. This explained so much. Chase sat on the side of the bed, speechless. And then the unthinkable happened. Her phone rang. His heart was beating rapidly. It was Tim. Chase pressed the green button to connect the call.

"Hey baby, where are you? I thought you were coming over."

"Who is this? And why are you calling my wife?"

"Your wife? Yo, I'm calling Stephanie."

"And Stephanie is my wife." There was a long pause. Apparently the other guy was just as surprised as he was. Stephanie was deceiving both of them. Chase heard the guy curse under his breath and then there was a click. "Hello . . . hello?" The man was gone. Chase started to call back, but changed his mind. What would be the point? There was none.

Chase dropped the phone on the nightstand, hobbled to the bathroom and locked the door. When he heard Stephanie enter the room, he turned on the shower so that he couldn't hear her voice. He wasn't in a place to hold a rational conversation.

After about hour, he emerged from the bathroom. Heartbroken. How could he have been so ignorant? Clearly she was having an affair. It was so obvious. Yet, he didn't see it. Now the only question he needed to answer was where do they go from here?

That evening when Stephanie arrived, Chase was sitting on the couch waiting for her.

"I'm surprised you're still up" Stephanie said casually as she glanced at the clock. "I was sure your meds would have knocked you out by now."

"Steph . . . what's going on?" Chase got up from the couch and hobbled over to where she was standing. He had a bewildered look on his face. "Please tell me, because I'm at a f---" he stopped abruptly. He felt his blood boiling. He knew he was about to venture into an area that he dare not go and say some things that he promised God he would never say again. Stephanie turned to walk away, but Chase grabbed her arm and whirled her around so that she was facing him.

"Stop. Stop. STOP!" Stephanie screamed. "Just stop okay." She broke down in uncontrollable sobs. As the tears streamed down her face, Chase noticed that her eye was bruised. His eyes immediately lowered to her swollen mouth. There was a large nasty cut on her lower lip. Chase placed his hand on her chin and began to rotate her head so that he could see the damage.

"Steph, what the h—" he stopped and took a deep breath. Chase was fuming. Yes, he was livid about the affair. But that was still his wife, and his job was to protect her. "What happened to you? Did he do this?"

"That's between me and him. It's not your problem."

"Not my-- you're my wife."

"For now."

"What?"

"I don't love you okay. I don't love you, and I don't want to be married to you anymore." The fiery words pierced him straight to the core. It took Chase a brief minute to regain his composure.

"You don't mean that. I mean, what about this morning? You . . . we-"

"That was a mistake. I-I felt bad for you. You were so pathetic. It was pity s--"

"Don't! Don't say it. No man wants to hear that from the woman he loves." He said in a defeated voice. Chase rubbed his hands over his tired face. He didn't realize how much he cared for Stephanie until that moment. "So, tell me Stephanie. What will make you happy? I know it's not me," he chuckled. "Is he the one you want?" Stephanie stood silently looking at the floor.

"Yes, I do." Chase belted out a cold, hard laugh.

"Yeah? You mean you'd rather be with him? Someone who beats you like you're his--" Stephanie looked at Chase with a cold, hard stare.

"Like I'm his what?" She muttered the words as if she was daring him to complete the sentence.

"Like your his whore. Well, actually I guess you are." The words stung Stephanie so that before she even realized it, she had slapped Chase across his face. It was so loud it echoed. In that moment Stephanie was afraid for her very life, and she didn't know if she should run or standstill. Chase took a step towards Stephanie, and out of instinct, she took a step back.

Chase was so angry he could hit her. But he knew if he did, he would go to jail for murder. "I'm not doing this with you," he growled as he grabbed his keys from the table and headed towards the door. "And you better believe the first thing I'm doing tomorrow is getting tested." His heart pounding. "Dogs tend to give you fleas." He spewed flippantly. Chase paused, peering at Stephanie with cold, dark eyes. "For your sake you better pray that I wasn't bitten." He turned and hobbled out the room, slamming the door behind him.

Chapter 10

It had been three weeks since Darya had seen or talked to Chase. She missed him. They had grown close over the past few months. It was odd not hearing his deep, husky voice or seeing his mesmerizing smile every day. Sure, she could have called him or even stopped by his house to see how he was doing, but every time she picked up the phone or passed his street, she lost her nerve. She just couldn't seem to complete the task. Darya was ashamed. She was his friend, and she hadn't even spoken to him since the day of the accident. Darya's mind went back to the last time she saw Chase. Boy, was she frantic that day. She remembered driving up to the hospital, her hands literally shaking. She had tried calling Stephanie several times, but her phone kept going straight to voicemail. After several failed attempts, she left Stephanie a message letting her know what happened and where they were. "I'll stay here with him until you arrive," her voice soft and shaky. It just didn't seem right to leave him at the hospital all alone. When she walked through the sliding glass doors, she walked up to the receptionist.

"Hi, how may I help you?" The young lady looked up at Darya with a huge smile on her face.

"My friend was just brought in by ambulance." Darya looked around the room trying to identify the EMS team who drove him to the hospital. They were miles ahead of her so she knew they should have been there by now. "But I don't see him or the ambulance drivers any where. Can you tell me if he's arrived already?

The young lady nodded her head and asked for his name. She picked up the receiver to the black phone on her desk. Darya couldn't make out what the lady was saying, so she couldn't tell if they found Chase or not.

"Uh huh, yeah. Got it. Thanks Chris. I'll let her know. Bye." The young lady placed the receiver on the hook and scribbled something on a small piece of paper. "He is in the back waiting to see the doctor. Do you see that woman over there, standing beside the door?" Darya looked in the direction the lady was pointing.

"Yes, I do." She said as she nodded her head.

"Go over there and let her know you are with Mr. Peyton, and she'll take you back."

"Thank you." Darya turned to walk in the direction of the lady standing by the door. By the color of her scrubs, Darya assessed that she was a nurse. She had a clipboard in her hand along with a couple of manila file folders. The lady was short and stout with dark brown hair that was pulled into a ponytail. Her skin was pale, and her lips were deep red. To Darya the lady appeared to be sick. But she couldn't imagine a nurse coming to work ill and figured that maybe she only appeared that way because she wasn't wearing any make-up. "Excuse me ma'am. I'm with Chase Peyton. He was brought in by ambulance a short while ago." The woman looked at her clipboard and leaned over to the computer, located on a desk near her.

"Sure, follow me." Darya followed the woman down a long corridor. They stopped in front of a door that was cracked open. "I'm sorry honey, I didn't get your name."

"Oh, sorry, it's Darya Drukker." The woman knocked on the door and peaked her head inside.

"Mr. Peyton, there is a Darya Drukker here to see you." After a brief moment, the lady opened the door wide enough for Darya to enter. As Darya walked passed the lady, she noticed how worn Chase looked. She looked at his leg. His pant leg was rolled up, exposing his rippling muscles. Her eyes traveled down to his ankle, which was now swollen and had turned a dark, bluish black. As she walked around the bed towards the chair, she could see that his anklebone was not aligned with the rest of his leg. Chase's eyes were closed at first, but when she walked in, he opened them slightly.

"How are you feeling?" Darya whispered. Chase just shook his head from side to side.

"I'm starting to understand why they shoot animals when they're injured." He chuckled. This pain is unbearable."

"I'm so sorry." Darya whispered. "Is there anything I can do?" Before Chase could respond, the doctor came in.

"Mr. Peyton, I'm Dr. Reddington."

"Hi" he muttered. Dr. Reddington, uncertain as to who Darya was, asked Chase if it was okay to talk in front of his guest. Without hesitation Chase consented. There was nothing he wanted to hide from Darya.

"Well sir, how are you feeling this morning?"

"Not good doc. Not good at all." The doctor walked around the bed to inspect the injury. When she saw the bone, she told him that they would have to reset it. She assured him that even though it was going to be painful, he would feel better once it was in place. A male nurse came in to assist with the procedure. As Darya listened to the exchange between the clinical team her eyes widened in shock. The thought of bones popping and agonizing screams made her entire body quiver in an unpleasant way. She so desperately wanted to ask to be excused. In her mind, she could see herself bolting for the door. But the thought of leaving Chase melted her heart. How could she leave him all alone, during his hour of need? No, she wanted to be strong . . . she wanted to be there . . . for him.

"Mr. Peyton, now this is going to hurt . . . I am so sorry for this." Darya jumped to her feet and ran to Chase's side.

"Chase, sweetie, look at me. It's going to be okay, I promise. I'm here." She grabbed his hand and whispered gently in his ear "Squeeze as hard as you want . . . I promise I'll be okay." It was horrible. When it snapped back into place, Chase screamed out in pain. It broke Darya's heart. She rubbed his forehead and spoke softly in his ear. "It's okay. You're okay." Tears welled up in Darya's eyes. She fought to keep them back, but to no avail. She couldn't stand to see him in such agony.

The ride home was quiet. Chase was heavily medicated, and Darya dared not speak. She didn't even turn on the radio. She pulled up into the driveway and helped Chase out of the car. Even though he was drugged, he still had the cognitive wherewithal to climb the steps. Darya took his keys and opened the door.

"Darya." Chase mumbled her name like a drunkard. Darya helped Chase onto the couch in the living room. "Daaarya" Chase sang her name again. "Thank you for helping me today." Darya smiled at his comment.

"You are welcome."

"Wow!"

Darya paused. "What?"

Chase gently grabbed her hand and laid his hand on top of hers. "It's your eyes. I think you are the most beautiful woman I have ever met." Darya blushed as she slid her hand from under his.

"Thank you, but I'm sure that's the medication talking." Darya said smilingly. She took the large afghan from the back of the couch to spread it over Chase. He was so heavily medicated, she was certain he would sleep the rest of the day. As Darya bent down to tuck Chase in, Chase raised his head and kissed her softly on the lips. His lips were so soft and warm. Darya was in shock. She jumped back. Her eyes stretched wide. *What in the world just happened?* She thought to herself. "It was just the medication. It was just the medication." She kept muttering over and over again. But in her heart, she knew it wasn't just the medication. There was an attraction. And she knew that if they didn't get a grip, things were going to get extremely complicated and very messy.

Darya was deeply conflicted. She knew there was no reason she should be. She was a born-again Believer who believed in the sanctity of marriage. Regardless of what society said, infidelity was not okay. She made a vow to her husband . . . in sickness and in health . . . until death parted their ways . . . she was his and he was hers. Nothing in her vows said that she should only remain faithful if he paid attention to her. According to the Bible, irreconcilable differences . . . moments of dislike . . . and extreme frustration were not acceptable reasons for cheating on your husband. And even though in her heart it didn't feel like cheating, that is exactly what it would be, if she pursued this further. What was she going to do? Darya was deep in thought when suddenly the phone rang.

"Hello?"

"Hi . . . Darya, it's me Chase." Darya's heart stopped. She couldn't breathe. His voice was so deep and alluring.

"H-Hi. How are you feeling?"

"I'm . . . okay, I guess." There was a long pause. The silence was a little unnerving. Darya could tell that something was wrong. It was in his voice.

"Chase? What's wrong?" He didn't answer. "Chase? You're making me nervous here." She said in a joking way, trying to lighten the mood, but it wasn't working. "Chase, sweetie, what's wrong?" Darya could only hear soft sobs on the other end. It broke her heart. Nothing was worse than hearing a man cry.

"Steph's having an affair."

"What?" Darya was in shock. *How could someone with a husband like this even contemplate such a thing?* She thought to herself. Oh how she wished Jeffery could be as attentive and caring as Chase. "What happened? How do you know? Like are you even sure?"

"Yes, I'm sure. She admitted it after I confronted her about it." He chuckled. Darya's heart was breaking. She wanted to help, but she didn't know how.

"Chase, I'm so sorry. What can I do? Would you like me to come over? I could bring you lunch." There was a slight pause again.
"Yeah, that would be good. I'm staying at the hotel on the corner of 24th and Limon st, room 534."

"Okay, I'll see you in an hour."

Chapter 11

As Darya exited the elevator, she glanced at the mirror. She ran her fingers through her dark, black strands. Her hair bounced perfectly into place and laid gently across her shoulders. She was dressed in an orange blazer and a brown tee-length, sleeveless dress. She wore brown silk tights and brown suede ankle boots with a gold buckle. The stiletto heel made her legs appear long and sleek. She thought that the bright color of the blazer brought out the highlights in her skin, which complemented the earth tone make-up palette she selected. Darya ran her hands across the tail of the rayon-polyester blend frock. She felt as if the lining was caught and possibly exposing her rear-end. She turned her back to the mirror and peered behind her to make sure everything was in order. It was. Why was she so nervous? She felt as if she could barely breathe.

534. 534. 534. She kept repeating over and over again in her head. As she walked down the long stylish hallway, she wondered what she was doing? She shouldn't be here. Darya wanted to turn around, run back to her car and speed out of the garage, but she couldn't. She needed to see him . . . be near him . . . and know that he was all right.

When Darya arrived at the room, she felt as if she was going to pass out. She clutched the bag of food that was in her hand tightly and took a deep breath. "Relax and just breathe," she whispered softly to herself. Darya lifted her hand slowly and gently rapped on the white, wooden door. Her heart was pounding. When Chase opened the door, the rhythm of her heart was so loud she feared that he could hear it.

His face looked tired, as if he hadn't slept in days.

"Wow, you look amazing" Darya blushed at the compliment.

"Thank you." She said smilingly.

"Please come in." Chase stepped to the side to let Darya enter the room. Darya walked past him slowly, her legs wobbling. Being near him caused her mind to draw a blank. She was at a lost for words. Talking about the weather seemed so trivial, but that was the only thing that came to mind.

"Um, I brought lunch . . . as promised" She gave a faint smile.

"Thanks, you can sit it on the table." Darya graciously complied and placed the bag in the center of the round, oak colored table. She placed her purse on the chair and moved slowly towards the couch. Her stomach was in knots. Darya placed her hand on her lower abdomen.

"Just breathe." She muttered to herself. As she sat down on the bluish gray love seat, she closed her eyes and inhaled deeply. Darya opened her eyes and exhaled slowly. She pressed her spine against the back of the couch and looked around the room. She marveled at the view. The décor was breathtaking. Normally, Darya did not like cool colors; she found them to be rather drab. She was naturally attracted to warm colors. She figured it was because they represented the spice of life, and she, at the core, was a bit on the saucy side. But the blend of blues, yellows and greens made her feel . . . calm and relaxed, which was something she hadn't felt in a while.

Chase sat down beside Darya. His elbows were on his knees, and his hands cradled his head. Darya could tell that he was struggling. She gently placed her hand on his shoulder.

"Chase?"

He peeped over his fingers. "I'm sorry," he said apologetically.

"No, don't be. Catching your spouse . . . that has to be hard. I'm so sorry that this happened to you."

"Yeah, but I'm not completely shocked. We've been drifting apart for years. I knew something was wrong, but I ignored all of the signs."

"Did she give an explanation?" He shook his head from side to side.

"No. There was nothing she could say anyway. She was doing what she wanted to do." He shrugged his shoulders as if he was shaking something off and pushed himself backwards so that he slouched in the seat. Darya thought maybe she would try to redirect the conversation.

"Do you want to eat?" She leaned over and grabbed the bag from the table. "I got your favorite," she said with a huge grin across her face. Darya knew how much he loved roast beef, so she got him a roast beef sandwich on a brioche bun and house-made chips from his favorite deli. Next door to the deli was a quaint little pastry shop that sold the best donuts in the city. Donuts were undeniably Chase's favorite, and it would be a welcomed surprise if she were to get him some. As she stood outside the shop, peering through the window, she thought about the last time she was there. They were working on a big project, and it was Darya's turn to do a snack-run. Everyone placed an order, and Darya took meticulous notes. Chase asked for some cake-like donuts. Darya inquired as to the flavor, but he didn't care. He just wanted a donut. When Darya returned to the office, she doled out everyone's portion of goods. When she got to Chase, she handed him a bag with three donuts in it.

"Um what's this?" Chase said as he rummaged through the bag.

"What does it look like? It's what you asked me for." Chase grimaced.

"What I asked for? I asked for SOME donuts."

"And that's what I got you?" Darya said with an annoyed look on her face.

"You only gave me three!" throwing up three long, thick fingers like a pouty kid. Darya shook her and rolled her eyes. "I thought you would at least bring back a dozen or so, that way I could share them with the rest of the office."

"Yes, of course you were." Rolling her eyes. "Ugh, do you want me to go ALL the way back to the shop to get you some more?"

"Nooo." Chase threw the little bag on the table and sat down to finish reading the legal document that was in front of him. Darya sashayed behind him, crinkling her round nose, "You don't need those donuts anyway," she mumbled under her breath.

"What?" Chase's head was still bent over the document. He did not look in her direction.

Umph . . . he heard that? She thought to herself. "Huh?" Darya whirled around to face Chase, her flaxen hair whirling in the air.

"Did you say something?" By this time Chase was looking at her. His elbow was propped on the table, and his head was resting gently in the palm of his hand. Darya shook her head incessantly from side to side.

"Nah-nope, not at all." Chase squinted his eyes as he looked at Darya. He heard exactly what she said. But he liked watching her squirm. He found it adorable. "Ahem." Chase noticed that Darya always cleared her throat when she was nervous. He liked the fact that he had that type of affect on her.

"You okay? Need some water?" He chuckled as he reached to grab the pitcher of water and a glass. Darya started to laugh and then rolled her eyes in annoyance.

"Whatever." She snapped jokingly. Darya turned to walk away, but suddenly came to a halt. She had a bewildered look on her face. She tilted her head gently to the right so that her left ear was slightly raised, as if she as listening for a faint sound. "Huh? Fred, you called me?" Chase laughed at Darya's impromptu comical sketch. "Yes. I'm coming . . . right now." Darya peered at Chase through her long lashes and gave him a devious smirk. And like that, she was out the door. Darya laughed at the memory. *Those were fun times.* She thought to herself as she opened the shop's door and crossed the threshold.

"Thanks." Chase reached for the clear, plastic bag that dangled from Darya's long, slender finger. As he removed the bag from her hand, his fingers brushed against hers. It was as if electricity shot through his body. "I really appreciate you Darya. You have no idea how much." Darya's stomach began to flutter.

"You're my friend, and I will always be here for you." Chase nodded his head and started to stare into space. Darya's heart went out to Chase. He was a good man; she hated to see him go through this. She leaned her body forward to give him a hug. But as she moved in, he turned towards her, causing their lips to touch. The kiss was unexpected, but it quickly consumed them. It was as if someone lit a match . . . no, an explosive. She wanted nothing more than to be his, in every sense of the word. She loved Chase. She did. But then her mind went to Jeffery. Oh, Jeffery. What about Jeffery??? At that moment, she pulled away.

"Wait. Hold-up. We have to stop." She said as she gasped for air. She looked at him apologetically, "I'm married." She whispered.

Chase looked away from her mortified. "I know. I'm sorry. I don't know what came over me." He stood up. "It's just . . . I've never felt this way about anyone before" he paused as if he wasn't sure if he should complete the statement. "Not even for my wife." Darya looked down. Oh how she understood what he was saying. She felt the exact same way.

"What do you want to do?"

Chase looked down at her. "What do you mean?"

"I feel the same way, and honestly, I'm tired of fighting it. Jeffery doesn't want me. He wants the church." Darya rose to her feet. "So let him have it." Jeffery looked at Darya in amazement. Was she saying what he thought she was saying? "I love you Chase. Just say the word, and I'm yours. I will pack my bags tonight." Chase couldn't believe what he was hearing. Could he finally be happy? Be with someone who didn't cower away from him? Have someone who longed for his touch and desired to spend time with him?

"Are you sure? This is a big deal." Darya walked over to Chase and grabbed is hand.

"Do you love me?"

"With all of my heart."

"Then yes, I'm sure."

Darya and Chase made plans to meet back at the hotel that night. She was going home to pack and to leave Jeffery a note. Then, in the morning they would leave town and begin their new life together.

Chapter 12

"Pastor?" Jeffery peered over the set of papers in his hand. His eyes were tired. He had been working on the budget all week, and he was exhausted.

"Yes Rose?" He said with a smile across his face.

"Elder Roberts needs to see you." Jeffery looked up at the clock. It was nearly six o'clock. Where had the time gone? And why is Elder Roberts out this late in the evening. He was an elderly man who didn't like to drive late in the day. Jeffery completely understood why and was careful not to hold too many evening meetings.

"Sure, please send him in." Jeffery placed the papers on top of the desk and got up to greet Elder Roberts at the door. "Elder, how are you?" The old man came in with a huge warm smile on his face. He wore large framed glasses, which seemed to swallow his small face.

"I'm good Pastor. I just wanted to stop by and chat with you a minute." Elder Roberts sat in the leather chair opposite Jeffery's desk. Elder Roberts was a soft-spoken man, so Jeffery sat on the edge of the desk directly in front of the Elder. This way he could hear him clearly. "Pastor, can I be frank with you?"

"Of course. Of course."

"Well, sir, I was praying this afternoon for the church, for you and your family. And . . . well, as I was praying, the Lord told me to tell you to focus on your family." Jeffery was a little confused by the statement. He was not one of those unfaithful men who ran around with women in the church. He was dedicated to his wife. He immediately wondered what rumors were going around attacking his character.

"Uh, well Elder Roberts, I don't really know what to say to this. I mean, I don't know what you've heard, but I love my wife, and I'm committed to her. I-"
Elder Roberts cut him off. "Pastor, no disrespect, but I think you're missing what I'm saying. I am not suggesting that you are unfaithful or that you play the field. Sir, Satan wants to sift you as wheat. He comes only but to kill, steal and destroy, and he's planning to start with your household. Tell me, do you love your wife?"

Jeffery thought that was a weird question, but he answered anyway. "Why, yes sir I do."

"Then son, focus on your family and war."

Jeffery acquiesced and nodded his head. "Yes sir, will do." Jeffery stood up and walked around to his chair.

"So are you going to stay there and work or are you going home?" Elder Roberts peered at Jeffery from over the rim of his glasses. Yes, Jeffery was the Pastor, but in that moment, he felt like a kid and he knew that he needed to be obedient.

"Um, I'm going home."

"Good decision. Have a good night Pastor." Elder Roberts vanished through the door. Jeffery sat at his desk trying to make sense of the cryptic message. It would be easy to dismiss it, but something in his heart wouldn't let it go.

"God, I believe that you still speak and that you send messages to warn us. Please tell me what to do." Jeffery could only hear Elder Roberts command to war . . . but how? When? Jeffery felt an urgency to go home. He wasn't sure what was about to happen, but he felt in his heart that it was going to be big.

Chapter 13

Darya ran through the house frantically trying to find her luggage. She figured she would take as much as she could and send for the rest later. She threw her large silver case on the bed, unzipped it and began throwing clothes into it. She grabbed her large overnight bag from the corner. She figured she would place her personal belongings and toiletries in there. Darya was so preoccupied with what she was doing that she didn't hear Jeffery walk into the room.

"Darya? Wh- What's going on? Darya was inside the closet. She paused. *What is he doing here? Crap. He's not supposed to be here.* Yes, she was leaving him, but she didn't want to do it in his face. She'd rather he not be here to witness it. It would be easier that way. "Darya?" He called out to her again as he walked towards the closet. Darya walked out with clothes in her hand. She was so nervous. She refused to look into his face. She didn't want to hurt him, and she couldn't bear to see him in pain. Darya threw the clothes onto the bed and began folding them. "Darya!" Jeffery shouted, grabbing her arm and swinging her body towards him. "What in God's name is going on here?" His eyes were dark. He looked so confused. "Baby, what are you doing?"

"I'm-" Darya looked down. This was so much harder than she expected. "I'm leaving you." Tears started to well in Darya's eyes. She turned away.

"What! Why?" Jeffery was stunned.

"Because you don't love me anymore . . . and I don't want to live like that . . . without love. I want more for my life." Darya began to cry. Jeffery was speechless. What was happening here? Where did Darya get this idea that he didn't love her? Of course he loved her. He just told her . . . no wait. He didn't. He hadn't told her in while. In fact, he kept canceling every trip or date they planned. He worked late all the time, and when they were together, they seemed to always end up arguing. Immediately he thought back to Elder Roberts' cryptic message . . . focus on your family and war. In that moment, Jeffery realized that he spent so much time focusing on the church that he neglected his wife. Jeffery plopped on the bed. If the devil destroyed his family, it was because he gave him the ammunition to do it.

"Darya, I do love you, with all of my heart. And I can't imagine my world without you." Jeffery sobbed. Darya walked over to where he was sitting and knelt beside him.

"Really? Don't play with my emotions. Do you really love . . . me?"

"Baby, yes. I know I have been neglecting you. Well, I know now. I- I was so focused on fulfilling my role as a pastor that I neglected my other role, to be your husband. Darya, I'm not just called to be a Pastor. I'm also called to be your husband. God will get no glory in my doing one and neglecting the other. " Jeffery placed his hand on top of Darya's head. "I'm so sorry I didn't war for our family. I'm so sorry that I neglected my job as your husband." Darya couldn't believe what she was hearing. It was like music to her ears. Tears began to stream from Darya's eyes. "Can you forgive me and give me another chance?" Darya shook her head incessantly.

"Yes. Yes, I can because I love you, and that's the true power of love." Darya and Jeffery sealed their exchange with a kiss.

Chapter 14

Chase went down to the bar to get something to drink. He wasn't expecting
Darya until later that evening and he needed a change of scenery to clear his
head. He climbed onto an empty stool and ordered a soda. The bar was
virtually empty, but Chase didn't mind. He needed silence. Chase was
about to start watching a game on the television when he noticed a woman
sitting next to him sobbing. He kept telling himself that it wasn't his
problem, but he just couldn't seem to block her out.

"Excuse me ma'am" Chase reached out his hand to give the lady some
tissues. "You look like you could use these," he said with a huge smile.

"Thank you," she whimpered as she took the tissues from his hand.

"I know you don't know me, but you seem really upset. Is there anything I
can do or anyone I can call for you?" The lady looked up at Chase with
sadness in her eyes and shook her head no.

"My husband left me for another woman."

"Wow, so sorry to hear that"

"Not as sorry as I am having to say it. Funny thing is, I gave up everything
for him and now I have nothing, not even him."

"Really?"

"Yeah. I'm so ashamed. I worked in ministry. I knew God called me to be
there, but he wasn't happy so I left. Took a regular job, and he still wasn't
happy. Guess that's what I get for putting him before God. Obedience is the
best sacrifice." Chase's ears perked up at her comment.

"What do you mean?"

The woman turned around on her stool to face Chase. "1 Samuel 15. See, God gave Saul specific instructions. But Saul, being Saul, only obeyed part of it. This caused him to be rejected by God. And when you're rejected, you open yourself up to a world of hurt. God wanted me in ministry. My husband wanted me to do something else, so I left ministry. Sure, I was still a Believer. I still went to church and was somewhat active. But I wasn't doing exactly what God told me to do. I was obeying what my husband wanted me to do." Chase sat there, processing the woman's words. He felt God nudging at his heart. Had he put Stephanie before God? He didn't think he did. He was only trying to have a happy household. But how can a home be happy without God being the first priority? Then to make matters worse, he was now causing someone else to be disobedient. What was he doing? He couldn't let Darya mess up her life and her relationship with Christ for him. It would only cause them to be in a world of pain.

Chase paid the bartender for his drink and said goodbye to the woman seated beside him. He knew that God had orchestrated this meeting, and it was his duty to correct the mistakes that he had made. When he arrived to his room, he packed his clothes and checked out. He was going back to the church he left. God called him to be a minister, and he needed to redeem the time. As he pulled out of the garage, he called Darya, but the phone when straight to voicemail. He left her a message explaining that he was leaving town and wouldn't be back. He thanked her for being his friend, but he knew he needed to do the right thing.

Chase didn't know what the future had in store, but he knew as long as God was first, it would all be okay in the end.

Epilogue

"Daaade. Daaadeeeee" Chara whispered as she hovered over her father's large frame. She peered into his face, hoping for a sign of life. Disappointed by the lack there of, she called him again, "Daaaadee get up," poking him incessantly. Chara moaned in frustration. She rolled onto her back, sprawling her tiny body across her father's hard exterior. Chase, pulling himself out of a deep sleep attempted to lift his head, but failed horribly. Chara's head was heavier than it looked. Her dark, tight curls covered his unshaven face. He brushed her hair from his eyes so that he could see, and he managed to peep one eye open.

"Chara? What are you doing?" He said in a groggy voice as he gently rolled his precocious three year-old off of his chest and onto the bed.

"I want panny takes" she whined. Saturday was the only day during the week that Chase could sleep in until 9 a.m. Well that was until his beautiful little girl was born. She didn't know what sleeping in was. Chara had on her favorite pink and white fitted pajamas. The pants and sleeves hugged her extremities tightly. Pictures of cartoon princesses danced across her torso, as she wiggled her small frame against her dad's warm body. Her white, furry, bunny slippers that covered her chubby little feet, flailed in the air as she attempted to mount the huge figure before her. "Daadee!" She whimpered as she shook him gently. Tired from the struggle, Chara laid limp across her father's body. She placed her small, round head on his chest. "Daadee please. I want panny takes." Every Saturday morning Chase made Chara fresh, hot blueberry pancakes. That was their weekend ritual. Chase was tired; he had a rough week. But how could he disappoint his little princess? She was, after all, one of his most beautiful accomplishments.

"Okay. Okay." Chase placed his hand on Chara's back. "But on one condition." Chara's face lit up.

"What?"

"Um, I need two kisses. One here" Chase pointed to his left cheek. "And here," pointing to his right cheek. Chara giggled in excitement. She climbed up Chase's trunk towards his face and gave him a huge, wet raspberry kiss, one on each cheek. "Mmm, just how I like it" he chuckled. "Come'on squirt." Chara hopped down onto the floor. She stood in the doorway waiting for her father to drag out of the bed. Chase slid his large, feet into his black, leather slippers. He looked around the room. "Where's your mom?" Chara shrugged her small shoulders.

"I dunno." Chase grabbed her tiny, mocha colored hand as she led him down the stairs. As he walked down the dimly lit staircase, he could smell hot coffee brewing. It was like music to his soul. He couldn't wait to get a cup.

Stephanie was standing by the kitchen sink rinsing a mug. The light from the window fell gently across her small frame as she sang softly to herself. "I sur-ren-der all" tears began to fall from her eyes. The past five years had been rough. She left God. Cheated on her husband. And ultimately destroyed her life. For a brief moment, everything seemed to be going well. She and Tim reconciled. She got a promotion at work that came with a corner office. It was great, well until it wasn't. Even though she had everything she thought she wanted, she felt . . . nothing. Complete emptiness. It was like she was dead inside. One day, when she was at her lowest, she was standing in line at her favorite café, waiting on her order. As she stood there, she started to scroll through her emails. There was nothing pressing that needed her attention. But she was bored and needed a distraction. Then she heard the sound of laughing. It was faint in the sea of voices that surrounded her, but it was enough to get her attention. As she looked up to see where the sound was coming from, she noticed two ladies sitting at a nearby table.

"You know I was in this really dark place. Nothing seemed to bring me satisfaction. I was frustrated all the time . . . it was like I had no inner peace." The tall, slender lady who was speaking was stirring her coffee. She looked as if she was in her mid-to-late thirties. Her companion looked as if she was slightly older, but not by many years. Both ladies were nicely dressed. Stephanie could tell they were business women, and assumed they were having a little girl time before starting their busy day at work. As the lady spoke, her friend sat on the edge of her seat, listening attentively. "One day, I just asked God, 'What is going on? What is wrong with me?' And in that moment, I looked down and saw this devotional on the table. I wasn't sure where it came from . . . it wasn't mine, but I felt led to open it. The reading for the day was Matthew 11:28. In the Amplified it says, "Come to Me, all who are weary and heavily burdened [by religious rituals that provide no peace], and I will give you rest [refreshing your souls with salvation]".   The woman stopped stirring her coffee and peered at her friend intently. "I've read this passage many times. But I never realized the purpose for Jesus' comment until that day." She gave a slight smile as she gently stirred the hot liquid in her cup. "The scripture says that Jesus was traveling to different cities, preaching and performing miracles. In other words, He was offering people both physical and spiritual freedom. Apparently, the people were eager to accept the physical gifts that Jesus bestowed upon them." She shrugged her shoulders slightly as she reclined back in her chair. "I mean, who wouldn't want to be free from daily ills, hurts and challenges?" As she reflected, she sat back up in her seat, thrusting her body forward so that her elbows rested on the table. "But they failed to realize that the purpose of His visit wasn't about their physical nature, it was about their spiritual state. He wanted to bring a life change to them. The physical healings were great, but they were just icing on the cake." She looked at her friend, tears in her eyes. "They missed the entire point. He was trying to give them something that wouldn't just cure their physical ailments, but permanently heal their souls. Jesus wanted to take away the burdensome load that they were dragging behind them like worn-out luggage. This is why He told them in verse 28 to turn to Him. He wanted them to know that if they were tired, broke-down, frazzled and frayed all they needed to do was let Him in; He could give them the rest that their souls desperately needed." Tears began to slowly trickle down her soft, pale cheeks. "In that moment, I felt like God was speaking directly to me."

Stephanie was so enthralled in their conversation, that she did not hear the barista call her name. On the second call, Stephanie's head snapped to attention, and she came back to reality. She quickly grabbed her cup and walked out the door. As she drove down the street, that scripture would not let her go. Was that her problem? Was the Lord trying to get her attention? Did he want to bring her freedom, but she was ignoring his pleas? Stephanie called out of work and headed home. She hadn't talked to God in so long, she didn't even know how to start the conversation. But she needed to talk to Him . . . she needed some freedom . . . she needed some peace. That day was the beginning of the rest of her life. She broke it off with Tim and started going back to church. She joined the worship team and participated in outreach projects, like she used to. It felt good. For once, she had peace and true joy. One day while praying, she told God that she understood that she was the one who destroyed her marriage. But made a promise to him that if he gave her another chance, she would make it right.

One cool, Fall weekend, she decided to participate in a community outreach project in the inner city. Multiple churches were joining forces to help the poor and underserved in the area. That was the day she saw Chase for the first time in over a year. Their eyes met, and they never looked back.

"Mmmm Coffee" Chase sang as he floated down the stairs. Stephanie quickly wiped her eyes and walked over to the coffee maker. She poured the coffee into the mug that was in her hand and placed it on the counter for Chase. When he entered the room, Stephanie's face lit up.

"Morning my love," she whispered as she leaned over to give him a kiss.

"Good morning you," he whispered softly against her lips. "And good morning you," He said as he bent his head down to kiss her protruding belly. His smile was larger than life. Words could not explain the joy that filled Chase's heart. Never had he imagined that he could be this happy. He could truly attest that God really does do all things well and that there was no power greater than the power of love.

www.ingramcontent.com/pod-product-compliance
Lightning Source LLC
Chambersburg PA
CBHW071451150726
48000CB00006B/2527